To Vanessa

First published 2011 by A & C Black,
an imprint of Bloomsbury Publishing Plc
50 Bedford Square, London WC1B 3DP

www.acblack.com

Copyright © 2011 Judy Waite
Illustrations copyright © 2011 Jo Bird

The rights of Judy Waite and Jo Bird to be identified
as the author and illustrator of this work have been asserted by them
in accordance with the Copyrights, Designs and Patents Act 1988.

ISBN 978-1-4081-4264-6

A CIP catalogue for this book is available from the British Library.

This book is produced using paper that is made from wood
grown in managed, sustainable forests. It is natural, renewable
and recyclable. The logging and manufacturing processes conform
to the environmental regulations of the country of origin.

Printed and bound in Great Britain
by CPI Cox and Wyman, Reading, RG1 8EX

recommended by

www.catchup.org

Catch Up is a not-for-profit charity which
aims to address the problem of
underachievement that has its roots in
literacy and numeracy difficulties.

Contents

1	Don't ask, don't get	5
2	Bad hair day	12
3	Be careful what you wish for...	23
4	A stinky idea	32
5	Soggy slippers	41
6	Blush and slush	51
7	Girl power	59
8	The terrible truth	66
9	Mopping up	73

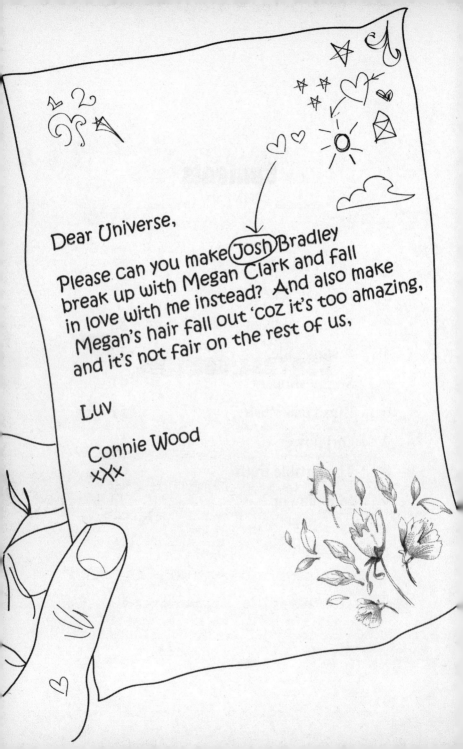

Chapter 1

Don't ask, don't get

Connie put her pen down on her bed and read the letter out loud. Then she crossed through the bit about Megan's hair because it seemed too mean. And anyway, if Josh was going to fall in love with her, it wouldn't matter that Megan had long golden hair.

Josh was going to fall in love with Connie. He would write her love songs, and play them on his guitar. The songs would be about how he longed for her in the dead of night. Every girl in the class would kill for 'Connie-style' boring brown hair. Even Megan.

Connie folded the letter, slipped it inside its pink envelope, and drew some hearts around the outside. Maybe the Universe got lots of requests, and Connie needed to make sure her letter stood out.

She hoped the Universe wouldn't be put off by the pink paper. Granny May had given her the pink writing paper years before, but she'd never used it.

Granny May didn't know about email and texts. But Connie reckoned the Universe was a zillion times older than Granny May, so it would probably want an old-fashioned letter.

"Connie? What are you doing?" Mum was standing in the doorway.

"Homework," said Connie as she quickly put the letter into her trouser pocket, next to her mobile phone.

"Oh yes? What sort of homework?" asked Mum.

Connie had to think fast. She said, "We have to learn this poem called 'I long for you at night'."

"Oh yes?" said Mum. "Who wrote that?"

Connie went red. "Um – Josh – er, Joshua Bradley," she said. "He's a sort of new poet."

"How can you learn a poem when you haven't got a poetry book open?" said Mum. She gave Connie a hard look. "Anyway, *I'm* longing for you right now. I'm longing for you to come and stack the dishwasher while I give Granny her bed bath."

"OK. I'm coming," said Connie.

She waited for Mum to turn away, then she got off the bed. Maybe she should have asked the Universe to put Mum in a good mood, for once? But then she decided it would have been a wasted wish.

8

Anyway, this writing to the Universe thing was probably all rubbish. Her best friend Katie had told her about it. She'd said her mum had written the Universe a letter asking for £500, and the very next day she won on the Lottery. She got *exactly* £500.

She went downstairs. She could hear Granny May grumbling as Mum washed her.

In the kitchen Connie began stacking the dishwasher. She felt her legs go wobbly as she thought about the song she wished Josh would sing to her:

I long for you at night,
I want to make you mine.

Only she couldn't think of a way to end
the song. Or at least, not a good way.

I long for you at night.
I want to make you mine.
Except you look a fright
And ...

Suddenly Connie's mobile bleeped.
Katie must have texted. She hardly ever got
messages from anybody else. She looked
around to check that Mum wasn't coming into
the kitchen with a pile of stinky sheets. Then
she checked her phone. It was Katie.

Connie sighed. Katie was probably going
to say that her boobs had grown another half
centimetre.

Connie was fed up of hearing about the wonders of Katie's boobs. Connie thought her own boobs were too small. She'd even started putting sports socks inside her bra, just to give herself a bit of a lift.

But Katie's message wasn't about boobs.

Katie's message was so shocking it made Connie drop the pan she was holding.

```
Hey Connie — hot gossip.
Josh and Megan just split
up. He's all yours now.
lol. xxx
```

Chapter 2

Bad hair day

For once, Connie was up before Mum.
She'd hardly slept. She had just been
lying in bed listening to the rain while her
head buzzed with what Josh might say to her,
and what she'd say back, and what he'd say
after that.

She saw herself looking into his dreamy green eyes, his blond hair flopping forward across his forehead. She thought about the song she'd dreamed of:

I long for you at night.

Well, that bit was true!

What should she wear? OK, it had to be school uniform. But still, there was some choice. Should she wear trousers or a skirt? Hair up, or down? Tie or no tie? But she might get in trouble if she didn't have a tie on.

At least it had stopped raining. Rain always made her hair go frizzy, and Josh was obviously into hair. That was probably what had made him love Megan in the first place.

Connie was just about to put the sports socks in her bra when she saw Mum standing at the door.

"Connie?" said Mum. "Have you got an exam or something? Why are you up so early?"

"Oh! Mum! Hi..." Connie pretended to sniff the socks. "Just checking to see if these are stinky or not."

Mum gave a tired sigh. "If you'd put your dirty things in the laundry rather than leaving them under your bed, you'd *know* which were the clean socks."

Connie gave up on the socks idea. She wasn't going to let Mum get her down.

Not today. Not on the day Josh Bradley was going to realise he couldn't get through another second of his life without her.

"You're not planning on wearing that skirt, are you?" said Mum. "You'll be warmer in trousers. And why haven't you put your school tie on? Do it now. While I'm watching!"

"Leave me alone, Mum," said Connie crossly. "How would you like it if I watched *you* get dressed?"

"That's enough cheek," said Mum. "I'm going to wake Granny, so you get downstairs and sort out breakfast. And no messing around on the way home today," she warned.

"You need to Granny-sit because I'm booked to do a haircut in town. It's a new client, so I mustn't be late."

Thirty minutes later, Connie escaped from the house. She ran down the wet road to meet Katie, who was waiting outside her own house.

"Do you think I should go up to Josh, or wait for him to come to me?" Connie asked, as they walked along the road to school.

"He's got to come to you. Boys like the thrill of the chase." Katie stooped to check her face in the wing mirror of a parked car. She pouted, and pulled a red lip gloss from her pocket.

Connie watched Katie as she smeared it on, sucking her lips to spread the colour. Katie's boobs even showed under her jacket. Connie wished she *had* put the socks down her bra.

"But if the Universe is making everything go right for me then Josh should be *longing* for me, and we'll run forward to meet each other in a slow-motion way," Connie said. "Like they do in films."

"Maybe," said Katie. "Or maybe the Universe will expect you to do some of the work."

"Oh no! Do you think so?" Connie wished she had put more details in her letter to the Universe. She'd left all sorts of gaps.

Katie beamed a fake smile at a group of Year Ten boys who seemed to be playing a game called 'push your mate over in a puddle'.

That was another thing Connie liked about Josh Bradley. He wasn't the 'hang around in a gang' type. He was in a band, and that seemed to set him apart from the rest.

I long for you at night.
I think of you each day.
I crave your dazzling light.
I...

"Hey Connie, guess who's behind us." Katie gave Connie a hard nudge.

Connie's heart seemed to twist. Her face burned. Katie must mean Josh. She wanted to turn round and smile. To do the slow-motion running thing. But her legs felt wobbly.

What if the Universe idea wasn't true? Perhaps Josh had just dumped Megan by chance. What if Connie rushed into his arms, only to find he wasn't her destiny after all?

He might be disgusted. He might want to push *her* in that puddle with the Year Ten boys.

"I feel sick. Help me. I don't know what to do." Connie gripped Katie's arm.

"You don't need to do anything," Katie whispered. "Just wait, and watch."

Connie could hear the footsteps.

They were quick. Not quite running, but not slow motion. She felt a flood of relief. He couldn't keep away from her. He was racing to be near her. And the Universe was making sure he was the one doing the chasing.

He was getting close.

Connie wondered if her heart would actually stop beating with the mix of fear and excitement.

And then suddenly the footsteps were going past her. It wasn't Josh Bradley at all. It was Megan. And there was something wrong with her.

It wasn't raining but Megan was holding an umbrella low over her head, so it was hard to see.

But this wasn't something Connie would miss. Megan's hair was gone. As if it had just fallen out overnight.

Connie gave a gasp. This was her fault.

She'd changed her mind about the 'making Megan's hair fall out' bit in her letter, but perhaps she had been too late. The Universe must do things as soon as you asked for them. It didn't matter if you wanted something good or something bad. The minute you asked for it, there was no going back.

But how could Connie let Josh Bradley gaze into her eyes, when she'd done something so wicked to his ex-girlfriend?

Chapter 3

Be careful what you wish for...

The first lesson was English. Katie was not in the same group as Connie.

Megan always sat in front of her with Josh, but today his seat was empty. Megan was on her own.

Connie hoped Miss Smith wouldn't make her sit with Megan. That would be so, so cruel.

But being behind her was cruel too.

There wasn't even a hint of what had once been Megan's magical golden curls. What was left looked hacked at. A real mess.

Connie wondered if Megan had woken up that morning and found her curls lying on the pillow? Or maybe she'd washed her hair last night, and it had fallen out.

She could hear the class whispering. She could see them nudging each other. They were all staring at Megan.

Megan sat with her back very straight.

Connie could see she was trying to be strong. She felt terrible.

"Joshua Bradley, you're late!" Miss Smith said as Josh came in to the room.

"Sorry, Miss," Josh said brightly.

Megan seemed to flinch at the sound of his voice.

"Sit down, Joshua," said Miss Smith. "There's a chair at the front here. Next to Megan."

Connie didn't look round, but she could hear Josh coming closer.

Then Connie heard Josh say, "Is it OK if I sit here?" He put his hand on her shoulder. Connie felt a warm glow.

"You could…" she began to say, "but – er – Megan's got a place next to her..."

"It's not Megan I want to sit next to. It's you," said Josh.

Connie looked up at the boy of a million magical dreams. He smiled, and winked at her.

"Joshua! Please *sit down*!" said Miss Smith crossly.

"Silly cow," whispered Josh. "She should keep her hair on."

Connie hoped Megan hadn't heard what Josh had said.

Then Miss Smith's voice rang out.

"Megan and Connor, can you pass these poetry books round? Page twenty, everyone. Megan, what *have* you done with your hair?"

"I was trying a new style," said Megan quietly. Whatever she was really feeling, she wasn't letting on.

"Well, I don't think that style suits you," said Miss Smith sharply.

Connie felt cross. Why did Miss Smith have to be so rude? Mum was rude too. Why did grown-ups think that it was OK to talk to teenagers like that?

Connie kept her head down as Megan came over with the pile of books. She didn't want to see the pain in her face.

"It's OK," she heard Josh say. "We don't need two. Me and Connie can share."

Josh pushed the book toward her.

"Do you want to hang out at lunch time?" he whispered. "We could go out on the field. Find a bit of space to talk in?"

"I ... I'm not sure… " said Connie.

"Come on, I won't eat you." Josh nudged her and grinned. "I've brought sandwiches. It would be cool to get to know you a bit."

Connie wondered if Megan could hear what Josh was saying. She felt sick.

She hadn't thought that getting off with Josh would mean hurting Megan this much.

"I don't think... " Connie began to say.

"Joshua Bradley and Connie Wood! If you don't stop that whispering together, I'll keep you in detention over lunchtime. Is that what you want?"

Yes yes yes, thought Connie. Anything to stop this terrible mistake.

Please, Universe, stop it, she thought. *This isn't the way it was supposed to be.*

Josh looked around to see where Miss Smith was. Then he nudged Connie again. He pushed a folded note over to her.

Connie opened it slowly.

I think you're hot.

Chapter 4

A stinky idea

Connie stood with Katie, outside her house. "He wants to meet me in the park tomorrow lunch time, but I can't go. It'll make things worse. But I feel bad about standing him up," Connie said.

Katie looked in her bag for the red lip gloss, and smeared it on. "Maybe you could tell the Universe you've changed your mind? Tell it you don't want a boyfriend after all. I'm sure it'll find a way to pass Josh the message."

"I've been sending the Universe messages all day. I keep telling it that I don't want Josh to fancy me, but nothing works. It seems that the Universe has made its mind up about me and Josh and it doesn't want to stop now."

"Shame," said Katie.

She looked over Connie's shoulder, then she giggled and flicked her hair.

Connie looked around. She saw three Year Ten boys riding past on their bikes. They waved at Katie and she flicked her hair again.

The boy in front wobbled. The second one swerved round him. The third one crashed into him.

"You idiot," growled the first one. But he kept his eyes on Katie, and waved again as he cycled off.

Connie watched them go. She was sure no boy would ever fall off his bike because he was looking at her. She ought to make the most of this Josh thing. But every time she thought about poor Megan's hair, she felt miserable.

"I'd better get back," she said quietly. Katie was smearing on lippy again. Connie wasn't sure she was even listening.

"At last!" said Mum when Connie got home. Mum was by the front door, her hairdressing box in her arms. "I told you to get home on time."

"Sorry." Connie pushed past her. "I got held up."

There wasn't any point trying to explain about Josh and the Universe to Mum. She and Mum couldn't even talk about normal things, like what might be good to watch on telly, or whether Connie could have sleepovers.

"I've done Granny's sandwiches," said Mum. "You need to cut the crusts off. And there's a pizza in the oven. I'll be back just after six."

Then Mum drove away.

Connie went into the front room.

Granny May was stuck in front of the telly, watching some kid's cartoon about a talking loo brush. Connie knew Granny May wouldn't remember it ten seconds after it had finished.

"Do you want a cup of tea, Gran?" Connie asked softly.

"Where's Karen? My hair needs a perm. Frankie will be here soon," said Granny May.

"Mum's gone out. And she did your hair yesterday, Gran." Connie didn't add that Grandpa Frank had been dead for five years.

It was funny how Granny May remembered him so well, and yet Connie couldn't even think what he'd looked like. Not properly. She went into the kitchen to get herself a Coke, and to make the tea. Then she went back into the front room.

Granny May took the tea with a shaking hand. She wouldn't even be able to hold the cup soon. Life – the Universe – it was all pretty cruel really.

"Where's Karen?" said Granny May. "My hair needs a perm. Frankie will be here soon."

Connie smiled at Granny May, and sat down to watch the cartoon. A scruffy mop was talking to the loo brush. But the loo brush wasn't looking at the mop. The loo brush seemed to have the hots for a red vacuum cleaner with false eyelashes and pouting lips.

Suddenly, an idea hit Connie.

The loo brush fancied the vacuum cleaner because it was flirty and pouty. It didn't fancy the mop because the mop was boring and scruffy, and probably smelly too.

Connie was fed up with a Universe that let people get old and forgetful, and was so bossy it wouldn't let you change your mind about a stupid letter.

She decided she wasn't going to let the Universe run her life. She was going to meet Josh in the park and make him *not* fancy her.

She pulled out her mobile, and sent off a text to Katie.

```
R U free 2mrrw morning?
I need a special sort of
make-over b4 I meet J.
```

Katie would help her to look as attractive as a stinky old mop.

Chapter 5

Soggy slippers

"No make-up," Katie said firmly. "That'll help."

"Oh, cheers," said Connie as she looked in the bedroom mirror. "Are you saying my face is so ugly, it's all I need to scare him away?"

"Course I'm not." Katie was behind her, pulling Connie's hair around. "It's just that he'll be upset that you didn't spend hours getting ready for him. Shall I put your hair in bunches?"

"I'll look about six!" said Connie as Katie lifted her hair out from either side of her face. "Ow! Don't pull like that. And they're not even equal sizes."

"Even better," Katie giggled.

Connie had the feeling Katie was enjoying this. She wished she hadn't asked her over. She could have easily made herself look gross on her own!

"Have you got any really old tops? We should go for the sack-like look," said Katie.

"My gran's got some horrible cardigans," said Connie.

"Fantastic," said Katie. "And has your gran got any frumpy old shoes?"

"Her shoes will be in the hall," said Connie. "I'll get the cardy from her bedroom first."

Katie thought Gran's cardigan looked perfect – if perfect meant really frumpy. But the shoes turned out to be too big. They slopped about as Connie walked. "Gran's feet have swollen up over the years, so Mum buys these extra wide ones," Connie said.

Katie looked along the shoe rack, and clapped her hands suddenly. "I've got it," she said. "Do you have any slippers?"

"I never wear my slippers," said Connie. "They're fluffy. And bright pink."

"If you meet him in fluffy pink slippers, I bet he'll never come near you again," said Katie.

Just then Mum came in. "Connie?" she said. "What are you up to?"

"Oh, hello, Mrs Wood." Katie smiled at her. "Connie's feet are freezing. Do you know where her slippers are?"

Ten minutes later Connie was out in the street, Katie gripping her arm as she steered her down the road.

"I don't want to do it any more. Let go of me," Connie said to Katie. The bunches bobbed madly as she shook her head.

The ground was wet from the rain and the fluffy slippers were getting soaked. Connie pulled at the baggy brown cardigan and wrapped it round herself.

Katie let go of Connie's arm. "I'm only trying to help," she said crossly.

Connie looked down at her fluffy pink feet. She had on wrinkly tights and Katie had changed her mind about the make-up. She'd pinched some of Granny May's pale face powder. Connie felt like a dead body who was playing at dressing up.

"I could meet Josh for you," said Katie. "I could tell him you're not well?"

Connie thought for a moment, then she sighed.

"The only bloke I've ever got with was Matt Langley, at Sara-Jane's party," she said. "He blew me out by text. It was the worst feeling in the world. So if I'm going to tell Josh I don't want to go out with him, I need to have the guts to do it myself."

"You could tell him that your mum is really strict, and won't let you have a boyfriend," said Katie.

"No," said Connie. "He might think that was romantic. Like Romeo and Juliet."

"Well," said Katie, "you've got to think of something soon. You're due to meet him in ten minutes."

Connie looked up the road to the park. Then she looked down at the fluffy pink slippers.

What if someone from school saw her looking like this?

And worse than that, in her heart she didn't want to dump Josh.

She wanted to run back indoors and pull the stupid bunches out of her hair. She wanted Katie to help her put on nice make-up. She wanted to wear her best jeans, and the new jacket she'd got in the summer sales.

At that moment, almost as if the Universe had decided to give her a bit of a nudge, her mobile bleeped. A text message.

"From Josh?" Katie said.

Connie opened it up:

```
Am leaving home now.  J x
```

"From Josh," she nodded.

"You still really fancy him, don't you? Forget feeling guilty about Megan. Let's go back inside and I'll help you look amazing."

Connie looked at Katie. It was so tempting. Maybe she should just give in? Let the Universe have its way.

And then a car went past. Connie saw a girl in the back seat.

A girl with her hair all hacked about and horrible.

Megan.

And Connie knew she had to go through with it.

Chapter 6

Blush and slush

Josh was waiting on the bench near the swings, checking his phone. He looked great. His blond hair flopped over his eyes. He was wearing a leather jacket and stone-washed jeans.

Connie's slippers were soaking wet. She hoped she wouldn't slip on the wet leaves. She could end up falling into his arms!

"Hi," said Josh.

"Hi," said Connie. She thought Josh would scream and run a mile when he saw what she looked like.

But he didn't. He put his phone away and stood up. "You fancy going into town for a milkshake?"

Connie looked at him. Then she looked down at the fluffy slippers which now had dead leaves stuck to them. Then she looked at Josh again. "Are you sure?"

But Josh already had his arm through hers.

He steered her through the park and out onto the road. They got to town. It was full of Saturday shoppers.

Connie was glad of the dead leaves. They hid some of the pink fluff.

Her ears were cold. The stupid bunches meant her hair didn't cover her ears. She bet they were red too. What was *wrong* with Josh? Couldn't he see how gross she looked?

"Wow, see that?" Josh nudged her arm. "That black car. It's a Lotus. I want one of those when I'm rich and famous."

"Mmm. Nice." Connie smiled, but she wasn't really looking. Her head buzzed as she tried to think of new ways to put Josh off.

"My band is playing in a club this evening. I'm the lead singer. When we're famous, every girl will want a picture of me for their bedroom wall." Josh bent closer to Connie, and put his arm round her shoulders. "I can get you in free. Maybe I'll sing a song just for you?"

Connie blushed. This was what she'd dreamed of.

I longed for you at night
I dreamed you'd sing me songs.
But now I'm really with you
It's all gone badly wrong.

"Maybe," said Connie. Then she made herself remember Megan's hair, and slipped out from under his arm.

"It's probably best if you don't walk so close. I've felt sick all morning. I might throw up."

"Girls usually get a buzz from seeing me on stage." Josh didn't seem a bit bothered that she might be about to honk all over his jacket.

"Actually..." Connie took a deep breath. "I've just found out I'm allergic to loud music."

"Hey, look at that." Josh's eyes followed a motorbike as it roared up the road. He put his arm round Connie again. "What did you say?"

"Loud music makes me ill. I come out in a terrible rash. I'd better give tonight a miss."

"Shame. But we'll put the whole thing up on YouTube later. It'll be an amazing show."

"I'll send you the link, and you can play it with the volume down," he went on. "At least you'll be able to see how good I look."

They reached the door to the milkshake bar. Josh dropped his arm from Connie's shoulders and she followed him inside.

"Chocolate milkshake for me, babe." He winked at the blonde girl behind the counter. "And a strawberry milkshake for the lady."

The blonde girl smiled at him, and flicked her hair. She didn't look at Connie at all.

Josh hadn't even asked Connie if she *liked* strawberry, but she didn't make a fuss.

"It'll match my slippers," she said brightly, as she took the glass of frothy pink over to the table.

"Look at this," Josh said, as he sat next to her. He got out his mobile, holding it up so Connie could see the screen.

"This is me last weekend. I got my mate to take it, so I can use it for publicity. My hair got a bit blown about, but I look pretty cool, don't you think?"

Connie wasn't sure if it was because Josh was talking about hair or because the milkshake was very sickly, but something made her stomach lurch. She stood up quickly, knocking Josh's milkshake all across the table.

"I've got to get to the loo. I really am going to puke."

Chapter 7

Girl power

"You mean, *none* of it worked?" Katie frowned as they crossed the road and walked in through the school gates.

Connie shook her head.

"He didn't seem to notice that I was wearing my gran's old cardigan and fluffy pink slippers. I spilled milkshake all over him, and then I ran out and left him on his own. I was terrible to him."

"And he still texted you, after all that?" asked Katie.

"Yep," said Connie. "He kept texting and ringing. I had to turn my phone off in the end."

"He must be really in love with you. He's not put off at all by what you look like," said Katie. "What a dream bloke!"

"It's not him," Connie said. "It's that stupid Universe. It's sprinkled him with some sort of love dust. I don't think he sees the real me at all. I mean, come on – most blokes would have run a mile just because of the fluffy pink slippers."

"Maybe you really do have to go with it?" said Katie. "Maybe you can't fight the power?"

Maybe Katie was right, thought Connie. The force was too strong. She would have to give in.

"Maybe I could just..." she began. Then she stopped. "Oh no, look."

Josh was by the bike sheds, watching them walk towards him. He held his mobile up in the air, and pointed at it.

"I bet that's the film of his Saturday night gig," Katie said. "Other girls would have been screaming and waving their knickers at him, but he was only thinking of you."

Wow! thought Connie.

And then she saw someone else watching her. Just a little way off, near the steps to the main doors, was Megan.

Connie stopped walking. She wondered what Megan knew. Had Josh told her he'd found someone else?

On top of being dumped and going bald, Megan had to deal with the fact that Josh was already head over heels in love with someone else.

"I'm sorry, Josh," Connie called, backing away as he walked towards her. "Don't come near me. I've got a rare disease. If you caught it, you might never sing or play again."

Josh carried on walking towards her.

"Please, don't come any nearer," said Connie. "I know you're talented and wonderful, and any girl would love to be with you. But I can't."

Then she ran towards the steps after Megan.

Maybe if she told Megan the truth, the Universe would back off.

She ran up to Megan. "Please listen to me," said Connie. "I'm sorry. I know you must feel terrible. But I've got to tell you how horrible I've been. Because Josh dumping you was all my fault, right from the start."

Chapter 8

The terrible truth

They sat down on the bench in the girls' loo.

"I was so selfish," Connie said. "I wasn't thinking about you at all. I'd fancied Josh for so long, and I tried this Universe thing. It was just a game really. I didn't expect it to work."

Then Connie explained about the letter to the Universe, and how she'd wished Megan's hair would fall out.

"I know a bloke like Josh would never really fancy me. If I hadn't done all this, you'd still be with him. And I could never go out with him now. It would be like cheating in an exam, and then getting top marks. I'd never feel proud, or really happy."

Megan stared down at her hands. "I think you're wrong about Josh falling in love with you," she said at last. "He's in love already. With someone else."

"Who?" asked Connie.

"You mean you spent a whole lunchtime with him, and you didn't find out?" asked Megan.

Connie shook her head,

"He's in love ... with himself," said Megan.

Connie stared at her.

Megan went on. "At first I thought he was trying to impress me. But it was nothing like that. He really thinks girls are falling all over themselves just to be near him. And to be honest, there are plenty of girls who are. I expect you're one of them."

Connie wanted to say that Megan was wrong, and that Josh really was in love with her, but then she remembered how he hadn't noticed the fluffy pink slippers. He hadn't asked her what milkshake she wanted. He hadn't cared when she said she might be ill.

"It wasn't the Universe that made us split up," Megan went on. "Josh didn't dump me. I dumped him because he was such a show-off and I didn't want to be with him any more."

"But what about your hair?" asked Connie.

"I was so cross with Josh. He never listened to me. He never even looked at me. So I hacked off my hair in a fit of temper, just to see what he'd do. And do you know what?

He didn't notice. Just went on and on about some picture he'd had taken for a publicity shot."

"But he must have liked you in the first place?" said Connie. "He must have asked you out?"

"I was a bit like you, at first. Staring at him. Dreaming about him. If I'm honest, he didn't have to work very hard."

Connie thought about all the longings she'd had for Josh.

"But do you know what I think now?" said Megan.

"What?" Connie asked.

"He's done me a favour," said Megan.

"I'll never go out with a bloke who treats me like that ever again. Somehow, in all of it, I've found some self-respect. There's only one thing I really regret."

"What's that?" asked Connie.

Megan went over to the mirror. "I was a bit of a twit, wasn't I? I've made a real mess of my hair."

Connie went and stood beside her. "I might be able to help."

Chapter 9

Mopping up

"Megan seems lovely," said Mum as she and Connie walked back into the sitting room. Megan had just left. "I hope she likes what I've done to her hair."

"She's over the moon." Connie smiled. "Thanks for taking so much trouble. I owed her a favour."

"It was no problem. I know I don't help you out enough. I'm always too busy, with Gran and everything."

Mum's eyes went misty. Connie could feel her own eyes welling up too.

The loo brush cartoon was on telly again. This time, it was a pop star. The mop and the vacuum cleaner were both waving from the crowd. The loo brush wasn't taking any notice of either of them. It was flirting with a band of feather dusters.

Connie watched for a moment.

The Universe had done her a big favour. She was never going to be a love-sick mop again.

She turned back to Mum.

"I don't help you enough either," she said softly. "It must be hard now Gran lives with us. Like having a baby again."

From the armchair over in the corner, Granny May called out.

"Frankie will be here soon," she said.

Mum looked at Granny May, then looked back at Connie.

"Not quite like having a baby. Looking after you was always a joy. I was never happier than when you were little. First words. First steps. My heart felt like it was torn out of me the first time you went to nursery."

Connie felt a warm glow fill her up. A bit like the glow she'd felt when she'd believed Josh fancied her, but a zillion times stronger.

Because this time, it was about something real.

She gave Mum a hug. Mum hugged her back.

"I've arranged for Granny to go into a rest home for a week at half-term," Mum said. "Then you and me can go away together. We haven't been on holiday for years. Where do you fancy going?"

"Oooh – China? India? A safari in Africa?"

Mum laughed. "Steady on. I haven't won the lottery. Just earned a bit extra from the hairdressing. I was thinking more of Butlins."

"Butlins will be brilliant."

Connie hugged Mum again.

"I'm going to make some tea for you and Gran, and then I'm going to my room," she said. "I've got a letter to write."

"A letter?" Mum raised her eyebrows. "I thought it was all texts and emails these days?"

"Not to this address." Connie smiled. "This address needs an old-fashioned letter."

Ten minutes later, Connie had the pink writing paper in her hand.

She remembered Katie's story about the £500 lottery win. She could ask for that. She could beg the Universe to let Mum win enough for them to go to China, or India, or on safari to Africa. But she decided it didn't matter. The truth was, she didn't care where they went. Butlins really would be brilliant.

She picked up her pen.

Dear Universe,

Thank you for helping me learn something about what boys to steer clear of. Thank you for giving me Megan as a new friend. And an extra, extra thank you for letting me and Mum get on with each other again.

Luv

Connie Wood xxx

PS – if you get the time, could you set things up so some fit boys book into Butlins for the same time as me?